THE RAVEN

Episode I "Origins"

Tobey Alexander

TAGS CREATIVE

Recite the prophecy, respect it's promise.

A burnt jewel,

A hell demons throne,

Both twins will meet a fight.

The Full Moon Society will greet them all in victory.

1

FATED MEETINGS

NUTHALL SECURE HOSPITAL, LONDON

Kimberley Mansfield was worried. Despite her outward appearance, she hugged the pile of files and paperwork to her chest as she followed the gruff orderly along the corridors of the hospital. It had taken her almost seven months of back and forth to convince the warden to allow her access to the prisoners as part of her thesis. That and the conversations with the ethics board had almost made her give in, but the cajoling from her tutor had kept the spark alive.

Now, as she walked along the sterile corridors, it suddenly felt worth the effort.

'You're one of the first to be allowed in here. Must have impressed the warden or something. She's not usually one for allowing other people in here.'

'I guess I'm, well, lucky?' Her nervousness was showing, and she silently berated herself as she moved to join the orderly.

'I'd hardly call it lucky!'

The orderly was in his early thirties, weathered and grumpy. His jet-black hair was swept back, and he had a cold unkindness to his facade. Kimberley was not unfamiliar with the type of people that worked in places such as the Nuthall. There had to be an air of disconnect from the patients, and this man was no exception. Watching his expression, they reached a secure door at the end of the corridor and the orderly set about presenting his ID card towards the reader.

'What do you mean by that?'

'This place isn't exactly the sort of place young girls should come,' he offered as the door unlocked and he pulled it open. 'Patients here haven't seen anyone but the staff for some time. I expect a pretty little thing like you might stir some attention.'

'Spare me the Silence Of The Lambs routine, but this isn't my first visit to a place like this.'

'Oh, I think you'll find it is.'

There was something about the orderly's smirk that begged for further interrogation, but Kimberley was cut short as they arrived at a second security station. Ignoring the conversations between the orderly and the security staff, Kimberley moved to the wide window that looked out into the main atrium of the hospital site.

It wasn't what she had been expecting in the slightest. The streamline and sterile modern interior was at odds with the normal dingy appearance she had become accustomed to. Often the places they gave her access to had occupied some aged historical building, but this, this was something different. Looking down, she realised they were three levels above the ground, with levels of secure accommodation and sectioned areas for so-called free movement.

'It's different from what I'm used to,' Kimberley remarked as the orderly joined her and thrust out an identification badge marked VISITOR into her hand. 'It's a lot cleaner.'

'We aren't completely government funded. We have the luxury of being sponsored by a variety of outside sources.'

'I thought you weren't a private facility.'

'We sit on that fine line between public and private. The warden's done well to get us what we need and keep us ticking over as we do.'

'Looks like she's doing a good job.' Kimberley sensed there was more to what the man was saying, but thought better than to press. 'Will I get to meet her when I'm done?'

'We'll have to see what her schedule looks like, but she is keen to put a face to the name.' Stepping back from the window, he looked at the security staff, who offered a curt nod. 'Shall we?'

'Who am I being given access to?'

'Ah yes, how remiss of me.' Stepping back to the security booth, the orderly picked up a paper file and handed it to Kimberley. 'The warden has selected patients based on the profile questionnaire you sent. You'll be meeting John Smith.'

'John Smith?'

'While he's brought up from *The Deck*, you'll have time to go over his paperwork.'

'I'm surprised it's not an on USB or something,' Kimberley replied as she precariously held onto the paperwork and tried to peek inside the file.

'Technology has its place, but good old paper can't be copied or taken away. You'll have to surrender that when you're done.'

'Can I make notes?'

'Yes.'

Opening the next set of doors, Kimberley followed on in silence and slipped the manilla folder into the pile of paperwork she had brought with her. After what felt like an age of security doors and airlock style thoroughfares, Kimberley found herself in a narrow glass lift that descended towards what the orderly had called *The Deck*.

'How many patients are there?'

'Last count, just over two-hundred.'

'It's a big facility for such a small number.'

'Trust me,' the orderly scoffed as the lift ground to a halt. 'That's capacity, especially considering how much help some of them need.'

On cue, the lift doors opened, and the air was filled with the chatter of voices and sounds of muffled screams. Kimberley was familiar with the sounds of places like this and while the sterile exterior attempted to portray a different story, the sounds echoing in the vast open space told her it was just the same as all the others she had visited.

'You can take a seat in there. It'll be about twenty-minutes until he's ready.'

'Can I see him in his everyday surrounding before I meet him?'

Pausing at the door to a small holding room, the orderly stopped short of opening it. Turning to face her, Kimberley suddenly felt small in his shadow as his gaze bore into her.

'Like I said up there, you're not here to upset the balance. The fewer patients that see you the better.' Pushing open the door, he indicated for her to enter. 'That's why you'll be interviewing him in the old wing.'

'Old wing?'

'More like what you're used to visiting. Now, if you don't mind.'

Not giving her any chance to reply, the orderly stepped back over the threshold and pulled the door shut behind him. Dropping her paperwork onto a small coffee table, Kimberley spied the coffee machine in the corner and quickly made herself as comfortable as she could.

Having poured a mug of what would undoubtedly be stale-tasting coffee, she moved back to the table and dropped into the plastic chair to pour over the folder they had given her. Unsurprisingly, the contents were light. The pages that had been collated were out of order and immediately she noticed from the first three pages, the numbering in the top right corner skipped from single figures to the high forties.

'Seems there's a lot they don't want me to know about you, John Smith.' Kimberley hushed as she flipped open her notepad and set about making her notes.

Lost in the file, Kimberley jumped in her seat when the orderly pushed open the door. Casting a glance at her watch, it surprised her to see almost an hour had passed since she had fetched the now lukewarm coffee from the machine and set about making her notes.

'He's ready for you.'

'Just let me sort my stuff out.'

The orderly loitered at the threshold to the small waiting room as Kimberley hurried to pile her paperwork together. As she scooped it back into her arms, the gentle flickering of a red light in the room's corner caught her attention. Mounted in the shadows, she noticed a small CCTV camera pointing directly down at where she had been sitting. Although it was not an unfamiliar sight in a secure hospital, the fact she hadn't realised she was being watched made her feel uneasy.

'It's only a couple minutes' walk from here and then you've got the rest of the morning with him. We break for lunch at half-past one.'

'And do I get to continue after lunch?'

'Yes. You'll have until three o'clock.'

'Thank you.'

Passing through a curious set of doors, Kimberley found herself once again in more familiar surroundings. Unlike the sleek lines of the main building, she now found herself in the tighter confines of a Victorian brick building. Immediately, the air changed from cool air-conditioned to damp and stale. This was more what she had become accustomed to during her dissertation research, and she once again felt at home as they descended a spiral staircase and found themselves in a narrow corridor. Imposing metal doors lined one side, while the other was plain brick with no doors or windows.

'This one's yours.' The orderly snapped as they reached the third rusted door along. 'I'll be down there watching on the cameras.'

'Ok.' Kimberley fought to hide her nerves.

'Please remember the paperwork you signed coming in. No digital recording devices other than cassette tapes and paper notes.'

'I remember.'

'Oh, and one last thing.' The orderly added as he slipped the key into the oversized lock. 'No touching.'

'Touching?'

'Keep your hands to yourself. Keep your distance from him and you'll be fine.'

'Why, is he dangerous?' Kimberley's heart pounded in her ears. 'There weren't any warning markers on the front sheet of his file.'

'Just trust me.'

Pulling open the door, Kimberley's attention turned into the small interview cell and what waited for her inside.

Silently scorning herself, Kimberley couldn't help but smile at her own foolishness. The orderly had done a very good job of getting her mind racing as they had made their way into the depths of the hospital. Seeing John Smith shackled to the table in the centre of the room, she was reminded how playful the staff could be. Walking into the room, she shrugged off the idiotic concern she had allowed to grow in her stomach and waited for the door to close.

'I must be doing something right. The warden never lets me have visitors.'

John Smith looked normal. Nothing about his exterior betrayed any of the ailments that had been noted in his file. Apart from looking in need of a good meal and a shave, there was something almost handsome about his appearance as he sat dressed in the drab grey clothes the hospital had issued him. Behind the blonde fringe that danced over his forehead, Kimberley could see his strikingly blue eyes as they looked up at her from across the table. John looked to be in his early thirties, but his eyes and the dark circles around them told a different story.

'Did they tell you who I am and why I'm here?'

'You're a student, doing research on long-term patients detained in the public healthcare system.'

'Something like that.'

'Please, take a seat.'

Accepting the offer, Kimberley lowered her papers onto the table and set about making the space her own on the table. Feeling his eyes on her, Kimberley chanced a glance and was surprised to see an amused smile on his face.

'Something amusing you?'

'Nothing.' John smirked and leant back in his chair. 'I was admiring your clothes.'

'I beg your pardon.'

'They're different from what I remember. All I see are white uniforms or grey ones.'

'How long have you been here?'

'Doesn't it say in that little file they've given you?'

'Actually, no.' Kimberley had noticed a lot of the relevant dates had been missing from the summary.

'That's not surprising. I can't imagine they'd want you knowing everything.'

'Well, why don't you tell me what you think I want to know.'

'Get yourself settled first. I expect you'll need to start that thing recording before we get started. I'd hate for you to miss any of the finer details.'

Kimberley felt like John was playing with her. Having experienced the manipulations of inmates in criminal, secure hospitals, she was no stranger to the games they played. Making a mental note to tread carefully, she allowed herself to appear calm and composed as she made herself as comfortable as possible. Only when she was ready did she start the battered old tape recorder they had given her and made her introductions.

'Right, my name is Kimberley Mansfield and I'm interviewing John Smith at the Nuthall Secure Hospital. Why don't we start with a simple introduction? Can you tell me how long you've been here?'

'Straight in at the deep end, I like it!' Kimberley looked confused as John leant his elbows on the table to look at her. 'I've been a resident of this place for going on thirty-three years now.'

'Wait, that can't be right. It says here you were born October third ninety-eighty nine.'

'No, that's when I arrived here.'

'It clearly says date of birth.'

'Well, that's wrong.'

Scribbling her notes, Kimberley couldn't help but stare into his eyes as he spoke.

'So, what is your date of birth?'

'April twenty-first, eighteen sixty-six.'

'Right.' Once again, Kimberley felt the fool. 'It says here you-'

'If you don't mind,' John interrupted without an apology. 'That's when I was born. What's even more interesting is the fact I died on the twelfth of November eighteen-eighty nine.'

Kimberley looked up from her notes, and despite knowing he was recalling memories of a broken mind, she could tell by the look on his face that John believed what he was saying.

2

TROUBLED PAST

'I'm sure you believe what you're telling me.' Kimberley knew she was treading a fine line. Anything she said could close John up and bring her interview to an abrupt end.

'What does that paperwork say would be my cause for makin it up?'

'The doctors have identified a number of diagnosis for you.'

'Care to share?' There was a nonchalant air about John as he rocked back on his chair.

'Surely your therapist has told you what they think you suffer from?'

'Schizophrenia, paranoid delusions, anxiety, autism, and a pinch of attention deficit. I expect they are somewhere on the list.'

Kimberley scanned through the documentation and found the diagnosis list she was looking for. Lifting the sheet from the file, she pushed it across the table for John to read.

'No physical contact.' The orderly's voice blared over a set of unseen speakers somewhere in the ceiling.

Flinching at the sudden voice, Kimberley looked for the source and then returned her attention to John, who simply hung his head over the paper.

'We are well aware of the rules,' John replied to the unseen speaker as he read through the printed list. 'Borderline personality disorder?'

'You disagree with it?' Kimberley pressed, seizing on John's intrigue.

Kimberley knew the dance she would have to weave in order to keep John engaged. This would be her sixteenth interview, and so far she had only gained material enough for her thesis from five of them. The others, as many did, opened up at first and then withdrew back into the protective shells they had created as a result of their disorders. Watching him read the page, Kimberley sensed there was something different. John somehow seemed more aware of himself and his surroundings than the others and yet there was something she could not put her finger on.

'I'm curious as to what it means.'

'It's a mental illness that impacts a person's ability to regulate their emotions. It's an extremely complex condition and manifests itself differently from patient to patient.'

'And you think it fits?'

'How am I supposed to make an assessment this early?' Kimberley was doing her best to be charming and John could see that. 'Maybe we can start by delving a little deeper into you.'

'I'm an open book.' John replied and sat back in the chair. 'You have everything you need to make your assessments in those censored pages.'

'Censored?'

'They're giving you pieces of the jigsaw Miss, what was your name?'

'Kimberley, but you can call me Kim if that's easier.'

'Kimberley it is then.' John offered a smile but it was impossible to read his true expression.

'You said this was censored. What would they want to keep out?'

'A very many things I would expect. I've been here such a long time I expect there are filing cabinets filled with their notes and observations, yet you get a dozen pages crammed into a brown folder in no real order.'

Kimberley had already recognised the mishmash of paperwork, but found it curious that John would be so perceptive. Balancing delicately, careful how to phrase her questions and come across, she pressed further with John.

'Would you care to tell me what you think they'd not want me to see?'

'You don't have enough time for all the details. The fact they've lied about my date of birth should have piqued your interest enough.'

'Have they though? Have they really lied or do you simply believe what you're telling me?'

'Why don't you tell me!' John leaned forward to rest his elbows on the table and stare across at her. 'You've been quick to accept the black and white writing while dismissing what I've said.'

Watching her cheeks flush, John revelled in the fact he was making her uncomfortable. Knowing the young intern would be as nervous as she had ever been, he couldn't help but admire the way she carried herself. Feeling the smallest level of remorse for being difficult, he soon changed his mind as she continued to press around his declaration about his life and death.

'It's more the fact I'm looking at a man easily in his thirties and yet you're trying to tell me you're over a hundred years old. Surely you can see that in itself would cause me to disbelieve what you're saying.'

'I thought you'd be able to see a little more when you looked. Clearly I misread you.'

'I beg your pardon!' Kimberley snapped. 'You're judging me on what, ten minutes of conversation and then judge me for doing the same?'

Catching him by surprise, John couldn't help but smirk as Kimberley fought to regain her composure. She was quite right that John had made his early assessment of her, and so far everything she was saying and doing was confirming his assessment. Seeing her flustered was somewhat amusing and very different from what he was used to when sat in the interview room. Normally it was one of the doctors that sat on the other side of the table, expressionless and simply marching through the torrent of all too familiar questions, steering him towards the diagnosis they were intending on labelling at the start of the session.

With Kimberley, it was different. John still had no clue why the warden had allowed him to be part of her research, especially considering the fact he had been locked in the Old Wing for as long as he could remember. Still trying to decipher this curious turn of events, John realised he had indeed adopted Kimberley as nothing more than another pre-diagnosis doctor and yet, with the simplest if pushes, she had revealed emotion.

'I'm sorry,' John eventually conceded as he looked at her. 'You're right, I've judged you and I was wrong.'

Whatever wind had been in Kimberley's sails evaporated, leaving her open-mouthed on the other side of the table. Giving her a moment to compose herself, John reached over and took a second sheet from Kimberley's side of the table.

'No, I shouldn't have snapped. That wasn't very professional of me.'

'You probably shouldn't, but it at least tells me you're human.' John offered his reply without lifting his attention from the printed sheet. 'Shall we continue?'

'Yes.' Once again composed, Kimberley lifted her gaze and waited for him to speak.

'So, where do you want this to go?'

'I'd like to find out more about you. Why you're here, what you know about what's happened to you and things like that.'

'I've already told you how long I've been here, but you chose not to believe that part.' Quick to compliment the remark with a wry smile, John didn't give her a chance to reply. 'Let's pretend that you believed me. What would you ask me next?'

'I'd start by asking if you knew what year it was.'

'Sometime around twenty-twenty, I would assume.'

'I'd ask you what it was like where you grew up.' Feeling she was being guided down the path John wanted to take, Kimberley knew better than to resist.

'London was a cold place back then. I remember winters being bitter. Sometime around my tenth birthday, I remember Mrs Creswell, our neighbour, dying. In my head she froze to death, but I think truth be told, she just had her time.'

'And where abouts in London did you live?'

'All over. My dad went where the factory work took him. But I spent most of my time in Whitechapel.'

Knowing there would be clues to the truth, Kimberley scribbled down notes as John continued to answer her questions. Occasionally, she would latch onto a phrase or word and circle it to come back to later. Having danced like this before, Kimberley's tutor had taught her to piece together the jigsaw pieces as a broken mind slowly opened up. Having sat through many lectures, she knew the pieces were scattered and while fanciful, there would be anchors to the truth in what John was telling her.

'Were you in the factories too, like your dad?'

'No.' John took a moment to draw the memories back. 'He wanted more for me than the life of a factory worker. I went on to join the Metropolitan Police, something my dad wasn't a big fan of, but it was better than the factories.'

'The police? What made you choose that?'

'A sense of purpose, I suppose.' John toyed with the handcuffs around his wrists. 'Seems ironic, all things considered.'

'I won't say I believe what you're saying, but I believe you do.' Kimberley looked up from her notes. 'If you're alright talking about it, I'd like to ask some more questions and see if I can't get through what you believe is true and find what is actually the truth?'

'Whatever you like, Kimberley, I'm happy for you to waste some time trying to decipher something that isn't there.'

'Did you have any siblings?'

'No, I was an only child. My dad got injured in the factory after I was born, almost killed him, but it meant he couldn't have any more children.'

'And your mother?'

'She was lost.' John struggled to hide the sudden wave of pain that boiled from his stomach. 'She did everything she could to support my old man, but she had her demons. The year I joined the police, they found her in the Thames, drowned in a drunken stupor.'

John fought to hide back the sea of emotion that consumed him. Grateful for the respectful silence, John watched as Kimberley scribbled a handful of notes on her paper. When she had finished writing, he had composed himself enough to carry on.

'How did that affect you, your mother's death?'

'I threw myself into work. Dad took it bad. He did the same, and we drifted apart. I found a new family in the police and wanted to make her proud.'

'I'm sure she was.'

'I'm sure she was a drunk who wouldn't care less.' John's sudden cold reply caught Kimberley by surprise. 'I appreciate the sympathy, I really do, but I've lived long enough to realise that she was gone because of the life choices she made. It may sound cold and callous, but it's the bitter truth of it all. Yes, at the time, I thought I was making her proud, but having had time to think about it, that was the whimsical dreams of an immature young man.'

'I think we should move past that then.' Kimberley offered, once again circling a word in the centre of the page. 'What about your job? What did you do in the police?'

'Maybe I should show you.'

'I beg your pardon.'

'I'm not blind. I can see your expression and maybe the only way I can convince you is to show you.'

'And how would you do that?'

Kimberley felt a wave of unease as John shuffled to sit on the edge of his seat and placed both his hands down on the table. Rolling up his sleeves, Kimberley noticed a jet-black bird in mid flight on his right forearm.

'What type of bird is that?'

'It's a raven, but that will all make sense when I show you.' John wiggled his fingers, making it appear that the inked raven was moving on his flesh. 'Take my hands and I will show you.'

'We can't do that.'

'Did you ask yourself why they told you that?'

'Because you could be dangerous.'

'I have no desire to hurt you. All I want you to do is believe me, and the only way to do that is to show you.'

'I don't understand how you can do that.'

Despite her screaming senses, Kimberley felt herself drawn to John's open hands. She had seen nothing in the paperwork, but more importantly nothing for John himself, that showed he would hurt her. Against her better judgement, she placed the pen down on the pad and moved one hand across the table.

'If you can believe I'm over a hundred years old, you can believe I have the means to show you.'

Almost reaching his hands, Kimberley stopped herself and met John's gaze. Hand still hovering over the table, she looked deep into his eyes and longed to see an answer. Knowing she was overstepping, Kimberley changed her mind and knew she had to bring the conversation back. Moving her hand away, Kimberley screamed in terror as John lurched forward and grabbed her wrist and hand in a vice-like grip.

'Let me show you.'

Unable to make a sound, the terrified shriek somehow lost in her throat, Kimberly felt the world around her close in as a wave of darkness washed over her. Like falling into an uncomfortable sleep, the world went dark and all she could hear was the sound of her ragged breaths as panic set in.

3

MEMORIES OF THE PAST

WHITECHAPEL, LONDON - NOVEMBER 8th 188

Kimberley sensed the darkness around her, and slowly her senses returned. Watching her on the ground, John admired his surroundings as Kimberley slowly came to.

John was standing in an open square in the heart of Victorian London. Painted in the pale glow of a full moon, the city was dark and dreary. Still dressed in his hospital fatigues, he looked out-of-place considering his surroundings, but none of the passing people paid him any attention. Looking up to the jagged skyline of pitched rooftops, he heard Kimberley groan and returned his attention to her.

'Take a moment. You'll be a little disorientated at first.'

'Where am I? What's happening?' Ripping open her eyes, there was a look of pure panic on her young face.

'Relax. I told you I would show you.'

'This isn't possible. Where are we?'

'You're in my memories.'

'Utter crap!' Kimberley snapped as she got to her feet.

Unsteady and staggering a little, John moved to offer her a hand, but she quickly retracted away from him. Eyes wide and senses overcome by her newfound surroundings, John gave her a moment to drink in gothic Victorian London. Feeling very much at home, John turned to look towards the silhouette of Big Ben in the distance. He had spent many hours reliving his memories of London, much preferring it to what he had last experienced of the city before he had been locked inside the Nuthall Hospital.

Closing his eyes for a moment, he allowed his senses to fill with the chatter of voices and the echo of hooves on the cobbled roads. He felt home, as if the city was somehow welcoming him with its warm embrace, wrapping around him like a comfort blanket.

'I need to go back.' Kimberley gasped as she clutched at her throat. 'I can't breathe. Please.'

'There's nothing wrong with you.' John sighed as he kept his eyes closed and turned his head to the bright moon. 'You're mind is simply fighting what I knows can't be true. Give it a moment.'

'I don't want to give it a moment. I want to go back.'

Feeling her fingers grasp at his back, John turned around to look at her. Still clutching at her throat, Kimberley turned away and stalked towards a crowd of young woman gathered outside the door to a quaint pub.

'They can't see you.' John warned as Kimberley tried to touch the trio of women but saw her hand pass through them like ghosts.

'Help me.' She screamed as she recoiled away from the spectral figures. 'Take me back. Take me back.'

Spinning on the spot, John closed her down in two long strides and took hold of her shoulders. Stopping her still, he removed her hand from her throat and held her gaze.

'Calm down. You need to take a moment to acclimatise to what's just happened.'

'I can't.

John waited. Knowing what it felt like, he had to let her body come to terms with the impossibility of its situation before she would be able to calm down. After what felt like an age, the expression of panic faded from her face and Kimberley once again regained a modicum of her composure. Enough at least to pull herself free from John's grasp and stare at him from a safer distance.

'This is London, the day of my death.'

'We've gone back in time?'

'Not at all, my dear.' John chuckled. 'This is simply my memory.'

'Oh, simply? Simply your memory. That makes it all okay, then.' Kimberley was fighting to keep herself calm. 'How have you done this?'

'We will get to that in a moment.'

'We'll get to it now!'

'No.' John replied, his voice flat and emotionless. 'This isn't the time. Now is the time to watch him.'

Beyond all realm of possibility, Kimberley turned and saw John Smith, dressed as a police constable, saunter into the open square. Looking somewhat cleaner and better presented, John had a handsome air about him as he walked towards a well-dressed gentleman standing in the shadows on the other side of the street. Passing by the three women outside the pub, they saw the approaching policeman and quickly scurried away into the night.

'That's you!' Kimberley exclaimed as she watched the alternate version of John move in front of her. 'You've not aged a day.'

'Why would I?' John scoffed as he moved to follow his other self. 'This is the day I died. You don't tend to get much older after that point.'

The fact John was so flippant caught Kimberley by surprise and she could see he was getting some level of amusement out of everything that was happening. Taking his lead, they followed to the meeting. As the past version of John approached the well-dressed gentleman, his face was illuminated for a second as he lit a cigarette between his lips.

'Inspector.' John offered as he approached.

'Mr Smith, how very good it is to see you out and about. Anything to report?'

'Nothing, sir. The streets have been a lot quieter, not to say I think we've banished the Ripper by any stretch of the imagination.'

'The Ripper, as in Jack The Ripper?' Kimberley hissed.

'Hush, just listen.' Motioning towards the two men, John returned his attention to the hushed conversation.

'The newspapers have gone quiet on the story. Fed, I expect, from the powers that be to return London to a state of calm.'

'But he's still on the loose, isn't he?' The younger John pressed the senior officer. 'Why hasn't he killed again?'

'That, my dear boy, I can't fathom. Such a violent spree and then nothing for almost a year.' Removing a pocket watch, the inspector checked the time and stepped down from the doorway. 'Do your rounds and be vigilant.'

'I will do Inspector.'

'Find me at the end of your shift. I have something I wish to discuss with you.' Before the younger John could press further, the older Inspector turned and stalked away along the now quiet street.

'I always wanted to know what he was going to talk to me about. I never made it to the meeting.'

'Why not?'

'Because, if you care to keep up, this is where I died.'

Despite the playfulness of his tone, Kimberley was still struggling to comprehend what was happening. As John set off in the wake of his past self, Kimberley pinched the back of her hand as if hoping she would wake from this crazy dream. Finding no change to her surroundings, she quickly made her choice and fell into step by John's side.

Struggling to keep pace, they moved with haste along the labyrinth of streets until they emerged into another vast open square, this time dominated by an impressive water fountain. While the shadows they passed were alive with movement and faces, wherever the uniformed constable moved, the people disappeared from view. It was clear that his presence was not welcome and more than once Kimberley thought she saw a figure stalking them from the shadows as they passed by the open alleys around the edge of the square.

'Follow me, we'll have an excellent position from over there.' John pointed to the churning water feature.

'Shouldn't we stay with him, I mean you?'

'It all happens here, and I would hate for you to miss it.'

The chimes of Big Ben carried in the air, encouraging John to move with haste towards the fountain.

'What happens?'

'Everything I told you will come to pass in this moment.'

On cue, a sickening scream pierced the air, and all attention turned towards a narrow alley on the far side of the square. The younger apparition of John froze on the spot and snatched his attention around in the sound's direction. Ripping the truncheon from his belt, he moved towards the dark alley with the weapon held in front of him.

'Police, show yourself.' John's voice quivered as he made his announcement. 'Step out from there.'

Standing a little away from the mouth of the alley, John waited for any indication the source of the noise had heard him. Getting no response, he inched closer and peered into the shadows. Nothing moved in the darkness. Somehow the shadows seemed darker and as he moved closer, the faint sounds of ragged breaths carried in the air towards him.

'Show yourself I say. Stop messing around.'

The shadows somehow grew from the alley, stretching like fingers from the darkness until they reached John's boots. Unnerved by the strangeness, he unconsciously took a step back and turned his attention back to the opening. As if growing from the shadow itself, a figure moved and took shape in front of him.

'Come out, slowly.' John warned as the enormous figure took shape in the shadows.

What emerged from the alley was not human. Although it had the shape of a man, the figure towered over John as it sauntered into the open square. Somehow the figure looked to be made of shadow and even the dancing light from the nearby streetlight could not pierce the darkness that surrounded its body. Putting space between him and the creature, John's eyes were wide as the figure changed and its features slowly came into view.

With broad shoulders and narrow waist, the figure looked powerful and imposing. A top hat was perched on its head and while the shadows clung to it, the features it allowed to be seen showed oversized muscles straining to break free of the ill-fitting

Victorian top hat and tails. Despite the ludicrous nature of a seven-foot tall giant emerging from the shadows in an ill-fitting suit, John could feel nothing but terror as he tripped over his own feet and crashed to the ground.

'What is that?' Kimberley gasped as the darkness melted away from the creature and its face came into view.

All charred skin and scars, a pair of lifeless eyes looked out from its sunken sockets.

'That is the Ripper.' John replied, his voice barely above a whisper.

'It can't be.' Kimberley protested as the Ripper moved to stand over the younger John. 'The Ripper was a man, the Queen's surgeon, or a butcher, wasn't he?'

'It was very much a butcher, but not in the sense they have led you to believe. That *is* the Ripper.'

Before she could ask any more questions, John on the ground screamed and scurried away as the enormous creature slammed a foot down onto the back of his leg. Hearing the bone break, Kimberley yelped in sympathy as the injured John grasped at his snapped lower leg. Fighting to pull his whistle from his breast pocket, John fought to squeeze it between his lips and prepared to blow.

Wrapping its hands around John's neck, Kimberley watched as it hoisted the younger man into the air to hang like a limp doll, his broken leg swaying painfully side to side.

'Do something.' Kimberley demanded as she tugged at John's arm.

'This isn't something I can change. This is just a memory.' John's attention was fixed on the Ripper. 'Just watch, as I have a thousand times.'

Fighting against the vice-like grip of the Ripper, the younger John managed to pull himself free and dropped to the ground. Unable to support his own weight, John crumpled to the floor, and the Ripper was once again upon him in a heartbeat.

'Who are you?' John stammered as he desperately dragged himself across the cobbled street.

'I am the darkness,' the Ripper replied, its booming voice echoing around the square. 'And you are nothing.'

Taking hold of John's leg, the Ripper hoisted him into the air as if he was weightless. Unable to fight back, John was powerless as the Ripper clenched its fist and slammed a heavy blow into John's stomach. Releasing his grasp at the same time, the younger John was launched through the air to come crashing into the ornate stone fountain at Kimberley's feet.

'Help him!'

'There is no helping.' John replied as the Ripper stalked over to him.

Something changed in John's demeanour as the memory played out before them. Reaching John, the Ripper dropped to its haunches and moved closer to the panting constable. Speaking so only John could hear, the Ripper offered its final words.

'Your death will serve no purpose. I have had my fill and this will be a pointless death.'

In one swift move, the Ripper delivered the final blow. Unable to watch, Kimberley turned away, but the sickening sound told her all she needed. The sound of bone crunching and the harsh escape of breath indicated that the Ripper had indeed killed John. Hearing the Ripper's footsteps moving back across the square, Kimberley turned her attention back to John's lifeless corpse at her feet.

Young, lifeless, and broken. John's eyes were wide and unmoving as the dead officer's body was bathed in the sickening pale moonlight.

'I want to go.' Kimberley stammered.

'Not yet.' John soothed as he looked down at his own dead body. 'There's something more you need to see.'

4

DEATH COMES FOR US ALL

As the demonic Ripper returned to the safety of the alley, Kimberley dropped down from her seat and moved to look at John's body.

'Why aren't you going to do something?'

Joining her, John took hold of her arm and dragged her away from the lifeless corpse. Struggling against his grip, Kimberley fought to break free, but stopped when a sudden rumble of thunder carried in the air. Despite the cloudless sky, there was no denying what she had heard as she scanned around for the source of the sound. Seeing nothing, Kimberley sensed they were not alone and expected the Ripper to once again emerge from the alley in search of them.

'There's nothing to do except to watch.'

On the other side of the square, something moved and as Kimberley directed her attention towards the movement, the impossible happened. From nowhere, a figure appeared out of thin air, a figure familiar to Kimberley, and yet it was something she had never seen before. The new arrival appeared on the move and walked casually across the cobbled square towards John's lifeless body.

As Kimberley drank in the stranger's appearance, her brain tried to make sense of what she was seeing. Dressed in a long, flowing black robe, there was no denying what it was. Carrying a scythe in one hand, tapping the base on the ground with every other step, this was Death. Arriving at John's body, the spectre of the Grim Reaper hovered for a moment before tapping the corpse with the base of the scythe. As the wooden handle nudged the body, Kimberley gasped at what happened.

While John's body remained unmoving on the ground, somehow his spirit emerged from the shell and rose to its feet.

'What's happened to me?' John's spirit gasped as it looked up at the visage of Death.

'Well dear boy, there's no easy way to put this. You're dead.'

Death's voice was oddly calm and matter of fact. From beneath the darkness of the hood, Kimberley could make out nothing of his facial features, and watched as John's spirit eyed Death with an air of suspicion.

'Just who the hell are you?'

'Oh come now, look at your feet and you'll see what I'm telling you.'

Dropping his gaze to his own body, John recoiled away in horror. Overcome with terror, John comically looked from his body, to Death and back again. Watching his reactions, John could not help but feel a wave of sympathy and embarrassment at his completely dumbfounded reaction. At last, John's spirit settled its attention on Death and waited for an answer.

'How...why...who?'

'Don't worry, this is an entirely natural reaction. Here, let me make it a little easier to talk.'

Pulling the hood from his head, Kimberley shrieked as she saw the floating skull in the pale moonlight. Illuminating the pale mottled bone, Kimberley watched as skin grew from the dark recesses of the skull. Crawling to cover the entire skull, all eyes watched as Death's face took shape into something more recognisable and human. A handsome man in his late fifties, Death sported a neatly trimmed goatee and rich green eyes that scanned around the empty London street.

'How?'

'Please, can we have questions longer than a single word?'

'I'm sorry, it's just that, well surely you can understand why I'm shocked?'

'You're not the first, and won't be the last.' Death smiled. 'But I'm here for a different reason than you might expect.'

'What is that?'

'I'll begin by telling you it wasn't your time.' Death rolled John's body onto its back and bent down to admire his wide-eyed face.

Seeing the moon reflected in his lifeless eyes, Death lowered his gloved hand to John's face and closed the dead man's eyelids out of respect. Muttering something under his breath, Death loitered for a moment before returning his attention to John's spirit.

'If it wasn't my time, can't I go back?'

'It's not that simple, my dear boy, I'm afraid not.' Death moved away from the body and loitered at the edge of the fountain. 'The moment of transition from life has been done. There is no way to send you back and yet your soul has no judgement to be made.'

'Judgement?'

'A long story dear boy, one for another time.'

'Then why are you here? If you're not going to answer my questions, is it just the fact you're here to take me to wherever it is I am supposed to go?'

'You have no place.' Death sighed as his fingers dragged through the water despite there being no reflection of him on the glassy surface. 'That's what has drawn me to this moment, to your death.'

'Speak sense!' John's spirit snapped. 'Nothing you're saying is making any sense.'

'Your lifeline was longer than this moment. I have seen you in passing and knew our paths were not destined to cross for many years to come and yet here we stand.' Death toyed with his beard for a moment before continuing. 'Whatever stole the life from you left a darker mark than I have seen in many years.'

'You mean the Ripper? He did this!'

'Is that what you call it?'

'It, no, him! The Ripper has been preying on the women in this city for the past few years.'

'That creature is not a him. That thing is a demon, born from the fires of Sub Terra and roaming the earth, feeding off the living.'

'Sub what?'

'We don't have time for an explanation of the world I Inhabit, just enough to make you an offer.'

'What sort of offer?'

'You present me with an opportunity, one I have not come across in my time as the Reaper.' Death moved closer and stood almost nose-to-nose with John's spirit. 'Being taken before your time, I have the chance to give you an opportunity to stop that thing before it kills again.'

'Then I'll do it,' John interrupted. 'I've seen what it has done. It needs to be stopped.'

'Don't be so quick to commit yourself to this. What I offer you is not a simply act of vengeance, I offer you the opportunity to be my hand.'

'Your hand?'

'I find it concerning that creatures like this can exist in the living world and move without leaving a trace, I can see. It would appear I am in need of someone with a connection to that world, and so I find myself talking to you.'

'Can I stop him from killing again? That's all that matters.'

'I will give you the power to face it, yes. Whether you succeed will be down to you. All I can do is give you the tools. You must put them to use.'

'Then I'll do it.'

'You wear that uniform well.' Death grinned as he replaced the hood over his head, once again disguising his face in the deep shadows of the fabric. 'Perhaps I should fashion you a new one.'

Without warning, Death took John's spirit by the collar and lifted him into the air. Rising like a spectre, Kimberley craned her neck to watch as the pair rose higher into the air above the empty square. Unable to hear what was being said, Kimberley and John could only watch as Death performed the ritual.

'Your soul is clean, untainted and too early for the afterlife.' Death hissed, his voice no longer calm and soothing. 'Do you swear to be the hand of Death, sworn protector of the living against the forces of darkness that would seek to disrupt the balance?'

'Yes.' John answered, his arms hanging loosely by his side.

Ignoring the fact he was now floating high above the ground and faced with the empty hood of the Grim Reaper, John closed his eyes and made his promise.

'Do you forfeit your transference in service as Death's Hand?'
'Yes.'

'You are to be reborn, my agent, my hand.' Moving higher into the air, the street looked tiny below as John dared to open his eyes. 'You are reborn, the Raven.'

Releasing John from his grip, Death watched as the startled young man dropped like a stone towards the ground. Dragged down by gravity and unable to stop the fall, John screamed in terror. Hearing his cries, Kimberley turned away, not wanting to see him crash to the ground. Instead of hearing a heavy *thud*, Kimberley heard nothing. After what felt like an age, she turned her attention back to the square and gasped at what she saw.

Where Kimberley had expected to see John's spirit in a crumpled mess on the ground, she saw something entirely different. No longer dressed in his uniform, John had taken on the appearance of the Raven. Dressed in a long black coat adorned with brass buttons, over a waistcoat and mishmash of belts and buttons, John stood proud and tall with a dark hood over his head. Turning to face the pair at the fountain, Kimberley was surprised to see his face concealed beneath an ornate plague doctor's mask.

'What have you done to me?' John hollered, his voice muffled by the leather and brass mask covering his face.

'I've given you the means with which to fight this evil.' Death replied as he lowered down to the ground. 'Now, do me proud.'

With nothing else to add, Death moved to the fountain and joined Kimberley and John as they watched the Raven take in his new appearance. Curious and unnerved by the visage of Death by her side, Kimberley chanced a glance out the corner of her eye and jumped as she realised the empty hood was facing directly at her.

'You'll enjoy this part, Kimberley.' Death hissed from under the hood. 'John remembers it like it's yesterday, don't you?'

'That I do.'

'I thought this was a memory,' Kimberley protested as she snatched her attention around to John. 'How is he speaking to us?'

'Some things just don't have an explanation.' John replied with a wink.

Kimberley was about to protest when she heard the familiar sound of the Ripper's footsteps behind her. Turning around to face back into the square, once again the shadows seeped out of the alley as the Ripper stepped into view. As before, the oversized creature walked tall and with an air of unshaking confidence. Bathed in the moonlight, the Ripper's physique rippled in the light and once again the lifeless eyes glared from their sunken sockets in the Raven's direction.

'What is this thing you offer me, Azrael?'

'The means to send you back to where you belong.' Death replied as he rested his scythe by his side and leaned back against the stone fountain casually. 'You displace the balance and I must return in kind.'

'A fledgling creature of your creation?' The Ripper chortled as it stalked across the cobbled square. 'A short amusement he will give me, I'm sure.'

'Your reign of terror and death is over.' John, the Raven, declared from beneath the plague mask.

'Is this some fancy dress parade?' The Ripper mocked as it came to a halt in front of him. 'Here I stand before you, proud and in my true form. And yet you stand before me like a whore at a party.'

'That may be the case, but I'm putting an end to your murderous campaign of terror.'

Stretching out both hands to his sides, a pair of escrima sticks appeared in each of the Raven's hands. Each of the weapons were gloss black with brilliant red lettering in an unfamiliar language. Testing the weight of the wooden weapons, he rotated them around and took up a defensive stance, both weapons pointed towards the Ripper.

'Oh, now this will be fun.' The Ripper smirked, its charred skin twitching in the moonlight. 'You should probably change your mind.'

'Not going to happen.'

'So be it.'

Twisting away, the Ripper was the first to attack as it lowered its weight and launched through the air towards the newly born Raven. Prepared for whatever was to come, John, in his form as Death's Hand, was ready to do what he must. As Kimberley, John and Death looked on, a fight between undead creatures had begun.

5

A RAVEN'S BIRTH

The Ripper's attack was furious and relentless. Having launched through the air, he delivered a powerful blow that pushed the Raven back across the square. Using the escrima sticks in his defence, the Raven halted his movements and raised his gaze to the Ripper. Having timed his attack, the Ripper lurched forward, dragging a powerful fist behind him. Timed to perfection, the enormous clenched fist slammed into the Raven's chest.

Too slow to react, the power of the attack launched him through the air, sending him flying into the stone base of the fountain. Crashing into the structure, the stone splintered and water cascaded through the jagged gap created by the Raven's landing. Soaked and shaken by the ferocity of the attack, he rose to his knees and peered across at his opponent.

'Why doesn't he fight?' Kimberley hissed.

'I am fighting.' John replied as he watched his past self rise to his feet.

Brushing off the water from his coat, he intercepted the next attack as the Ripper lurched forward. Deflecting the heavy fist, his return blow sent him rotating away. Slamming the wooden weapon into the side of the Ripper's head, the Raven felt a rush of pride as the top hat tumbled to the floor.

Taking a moment, the Raven took in the Ripper's appearance. No longer shrouded in the shadow of the tall hat, the Ripper's face was now exposed for all to see. A face of mottled, charred flesh. What had appeared to be hair was, in fact, a pair of crooked horns that had been grown over the top and down the back of his head. Turned up at the ends, the horns were ridged, giving it the appearance of slick-back hair.

'You fight well.' The Ripper snarled. 'Perhaps I should show you the true depth of my power.'

Clenching both fists, they all watched as the Ripper's body became lined with veins of pale pink light. Covering every inch of its body, the Ripper appeared to grow as the light moved up its body and into its eyes. Taking full advantage of the distraction, it once again attacked and barreled down a barrage of blows towards the Raven.

The fight raged across the entire square as neither creature of the afterlife was able to find advantage over the other. Despite the ferocious battle between them, the street remained empty of bystanders, leaving only Kimberley, John, and Death watching from the sidelines. Taking hold of the Raven, the Ripper hammered a trio of blows down onto his head, dislodging the plague mask. Tearing the leather mask from his head, the Ripper tossed it across the square and glared down at John's exposed face.

'Just a man.'

'Just a monster.' John snarled and drove the escrima stick up, connecting with the Ripper's chin.

Knocking his head back, forced back by the force of the blow, the Ripper released its grip on him and staggered away. Releasing a deep roar of frustration, the Ripper was quick to regain its composure.

'Call me what you will, this is my playground and no menial servant of him will stop me.' The Ripper pointed towards Death. 'You have sealed your own fate to an eternity of nothingness by challenging me.'

'He's done nothing of the sort.' Death replied from the sidelines. 'Now, if you wouldn't mind I'd appreciate you not embarrassing me by losing.'

Death's joviality caught Kimberley by surprise, but his words were enough to spurn the Raven to attack. Taking full advantage of the distraction, he moved with astonishing speed as he launched through the air and took the Ripper completely unaware. Driving the escrima sticks up and around, both weapons found their mark and forced the Ripper to go on the defence.

Shielding its face from the flurry of attack as, more than once, the sticks found their mark. So close to it, John could almost taste the fetid stench of death and decay that hung around the Ripper. Passing through the smell, he pressed on harder until the Ripper caught his right arm as he moved to deliver another attack.

'Fairer without these.' The Ripper snatched the stick from his grasp and tossed it across the square.

Moving to pull himself free, the second stick was yanked from his grasp, rendering him unarmed. Still holding his wrist, the Ripper slammed his head into John's maskless face, sending stars dancing in his vision. Fighting to break free, their combat became more brutal and desperate. Crashing his elbow into the Ripper's jaw, John heard a satisfying *crack* and, propelled by the momentum, John could pull himself free.

Spinning away, his long coat spreading out as he moved, John put enough distance between them and took a moment to settle his vision. As the world came into focus and blinking lights faded, he saw that his attack had dislodged the Ripper's lower jaw, which now hung at a jaunty and unnatural position. Taking hold of it, John could hear the sickening scraping of bone on bone as the Ripper returned his jaw back into position.

Not wasting time, John launched his next foray of attacks and this time allowed his newfound powers to take hold. Reaching the Ripper, John felt a sensation in his legs and launched the pair of them up into the air. Whatever strength had been contained in his muscles carried them high above the rooftops of the surrounding buildings. With the expanse of Victorian London in view, the majestic beauty of the moonlit capital almost distracted John.

Sensing another impending attack, John rotated over in the air and drove them back towards the ground. Forcing the Ripper beneath him, their momentum grew as the ground approached. Colliding with the floor, cobbles and roadway splintered by the sheer force of their landing and John was able to roll away unscathed.

'Good skills.' Death yelled his approval as the Ripper pulled away the debris that covered his torso.

Enraged by the sudden turn of events, he launched from the shallow crater and the fight between them resumed. Blow after blow, they fought with renewed ferocity until, at last, the Ripper gained an advantage. Wrapping its arms around John's waist, he was powerless to resist as the Ripper raised him over his head and dropped backwards, slamming his head onto the cobbles.

Pinned to the ground, the Ripper stamped down onto the side of John's head and pressed his weight down. Unable to move, John scratched and pulled to rip the dead weight free. The only release came as the Ripper raised his foot and stamped down over and over again until the world began to close in around him.

As his vision faded, each blow brought a memory flashing through his mind. The first he saw was his mother's body laid on the mortuary slab, her skin pale and soaked from the Thames.

Another blow brought another memory. This time it was his graduation into the police, a moment of immense pride overshadowed by the broken appearance of his father at the back of the room, unable to meet his gaze.

'I have no son.' His father's voice echoed in his head, bouncing around like he was right beside him.

'Time to die again!' The Ripper screamed and stamped down one last time.

The memory that consumed John was a series of flashing moments from the crime scenes of the Ripper. Each gruesome murder scene was etched in his mind, vivid and alive, as if he were there again. The women's youth and pain were painted around the room in scenes that were fit for nightmares. Knowing he had failed them, failed to protect the scores of victims that the Ripper would undoubtedly create, in light of his failure.

'I chose you for a reason.' Death's voice hissed, barely above a whisper in his senses. 'This thing will walk free if you don't succeed. I gave the power to protect those people, to protect those who cannot do it themselves. Now get it and end this.'

Feeling a jolt of electricity through his body, every nerve tingling from his head to his toe, John opened his eyes and pushed back. Whatever strength bubbled inside him was enough to break free of the Ripper's pressure. Moving the foot enough, John pushed away and rolled clear. Sweeping the Ripper's legs from beneath him, John snatched up one of the discarded escrima sticks and drove it through the air, burying it into the Ripper's chest.

Letting out a blood-curdling scream, the Ripper staggered away, clutching at the wood protruding at an awkward angle from its barrelled chest. Finding no purchase, the Ripper's chest glowed around the entry wound and John watched as its actions became more frenzied. Clawed fingers struggling, John could only watch until he heard Death's voice in his ear.

Appearing at his side, the shrouded visage of the hooded Grim Reaper leaned closer, so only John could hear his hushed words.

'Finish what you have started. Send it back to the shadows, free the living from this monster.'

'Why don't you do it?' John snapped, his attention fixed on the flailing Ripper.

'That is not my purpose. I transition undecided souls for judgement but you, you are my sentinel against the growing darkness.' Placing his gloved hand on John's shoulder, he offered him the discarded plague doctor mask. 'Take it, become the sentinel the world needs. Be my hand and do what I cannot.'

Dropping his gaze to the leather mask, John hesitated. Ignoring the Ripper, he saw his reflection in the blue tinted lenses covering the eye-pieces of the mask.

'Will I ever feel again?' John quizzed, his voice hoarse and dry.

'You are something else now, a spirit between this life and the next. You'll find a way to accept that.'

'Like you have?'

'Take it, become the Raven.' Stepping away, he left John admiring the intricately crafted plague mask.

Taking in a deep breath, John placed the mask over his face and allowed his vision to adjust to the blue hue of the lenses. As the smell of the leather invaded his senses, he made his choice and charged towards the Ripper. Still overcome with frenzy, it was powerless to do anything as the flesh of its chest now smouldered around the protruding weapon.

Reaching the demon, John drove down his weight onto the wooden stick, sending the Ripper crashing to the ground beneath him. Putting all his weight on the stick, it sank deeper into its chest. Pressing the hooked nose of the plague mask into the face of the snarling demon, John chose his last words carefully.

'Your reign of terror in my city is over.' John spat, his words filled with venom and hate. 'Go back to the darkness from where you came.'

Hammering a fist down, the air was filled with a deafening clap of thunder. The Ripper's body exploded in a cloud of black smoke, the force of which sent John flying backwards through the air. Rather than crashing to the ground this time, John landed with poise a handful of feet away from where the Ripper had been. As the smoke dissipated, John could only see the discarded weapon lying on the cobbled street with no sign of the twisted Ripper, only the tendrils of shadow retreating back along the square.

'Is it dead?' John asked as he turned towards the fountain where Death was sat.

'It was never alive.'

'Is it gone then?'

'That creature no longer stalks the shadows.'

'Then I'm done?'

'You already know the answer to that, my Raven.' Death clambered down from his perch atop the fountain. 'There will always be the demons int he shadows, and they will always need you to protect them.'

Before John could offer any retort, Death disappeared, leaving only John and the two unseen observers in the empty square.

'What happens next?' Kimberley asked as she looked at the John she knew from the hospital.

'This is where this memory ends. We should get back.'

Almost tenderly, John touched her cheek and in a heartbeat she felt herself ripped from where she was sat.

6

THE FEAR OF KNOWING

NUTHALL SECURE HOSPITAL, LONDON

Kimberley launched back away from the table, eyes wide and brow drenched with sweat. Wiping the back of her hand across her forehead, she pressed back away from the table until she reached the secured door.

'Calm down.' John pressed as he dropped his hands back to the table. 'You're going to draw attention.'

'Get me out of here!' Kimberley shrieked as she hammered her fists on the inside of the door.

'Or else shout like that and they'll come running.'

'Help!'

'Really, you're shouting for help?' John sighed as he slumped back in the chair and waited for the door to burst open.

Moving aside as the door was unlocked from the outside, Kimberley burst past the orderly and disappeared along the corridor. Leaning his head back, John looked up at the ceiling and let out a long, exacerbated sigh.

'Messed around with another one?' The orderly tutted as he pulled the door shut. 'The warden won't be so quick to let you have visitors again. Back to the shadows for you, John.'

Watching the door close, John kept his attention on the flickering bulb behind the plexi-glass in the ceiling. Listening to the locking mechanism secure the door, he waited a few moments before bringing his gaze back down into the room.

'Are you going to join me, or hide in the shadows?' John asked the empty room. 'I know you still watch me. How else would you have spoken to her in my memories?'

His questions went unanswered, as they always did, when he attempted to speak to Death. It had been a good number of years since Death had spoken back and while John could feel his presence, there was some invisible block between him and the one that made him in his image. Testing the strength of the chains and cuffs, John eyed the scattered papers that littered the table. When Kimberley had made her hasty exit from the interview room, a handful of sheets had tumbled to the ground. Peering around the side of the table, John's attention fell to a folded newspaper clipping.

Eyeing it with suspicion, the paper was out of his reach. Shuffling to the edge of his seat, he fought to drag the clipping back with his shoes. Straining against the restraints, John finally pinned the paper beneath the sole of his shoe and moved it towards him. When it was finally in reach, he scooped it up and unfolded it on the metal table in front of him.

'This can't be.' John gasped as he read the headline.

IS JACK BACK? NEW RIPPER STALKS LONDON

Reading through the article, what colour was left in John's face drained away. Every word filled him with a sense of fear and dread. Re-reading it, John learned of the latest series of grisly murders that had been reported by the police. Reminiscent of the urban legend of Jack The Ripper, the level of detail in the article left little to the imagination. All at once, the memories of the murders he had witnessed came flooding back. Pushing back from the table, John's eyes were wide with panic as the door to the interview room burst open.

'Warden's decided some time in solitary might serve you well.' The orderly declared as he stalked into the room, followed by two other staff members.

Grabbing the cutting from the table, John stuffed it into his pocket and quickly raised his hands.

'I'm not going to put up a fight.'

'Oh, please do.' The orderly smirked as he pulled an extendable baton from the back of his trousers.

Knowing what was coming, John longed to fight back, but knew the risks. His whispered oath with death meant he was to protect the living, not bring them to Death's door before their time. Knowing what he had once been capable of, John simply sat back in the seat and waited for the barrage of abuse that he knew was coming. The first strike came from the side and sent him crashing to the floor. Still shackled to the table, John curled himself into a ball and accepted the beating.

***

Kimberley burst into her apartment and stormed across the open plan living room to rest against the panoramic window. Now bathed in darkness, the shimmering city lights were hazy against the low hanging fog that had settled for the evening. Having hastily left the Nuthall Hospital, she had made it through the underground and found herself swept along with the sea of people in rush hour. Not knowing what to do, her head racing in a million directions, she had found a quiet corner and waited for the swarms of people to lessen before making her way home.

Even thinking about the impossibility of what she had seen sent cold shivers through her body. With her head buried in her hand, the screaming and rumbling of the approaching train had brought her back from replaying the disturbing memory of events. Boarding, she had made her way home and felt a wave of relief to at last be in the safety of her apartment.

Pulling a chair close to the window, Kimberley dropped into the seat and stared out of the window. Sat in the darkness, she looked at the flowing traffic far below in the streets and tried to make sense of everything. Snatching a notepad from the coffee table behind her, Kimberley set about making notes of what she remembered. Key elements, images, words spoken and, above all, the look of what she had seen.

As the hours passed by, she filled more and more pages with rough sketches and lines of text recounting what she had seen.

When sleep finally swallowed her, dragging her into an uneasy rest, the pad dropped into her lap with the last image she had sketched in smudged ink of The Raven.

'You were in such a rush to leave.' John's voice whispered from the shadows of her apartment. 'I'd have hoped to speak to you more.'

Hearing the voice, Kimberley's eyes ripped open, and she launched from the chair, dropping the pad as she moved. Scanning the dark apartment, her heart pounded in her eyes as she tried to shake off the dizziness from her startled awakening.

'Who's there?'

'Well, I would think that was obvious!'

'Death?' Kimberley's words were shaken and laced with terror as she scanned the darkest corners of the room.

'Not Death, just the curious man you left shackled to a table.'

'John?'

'Oh, come on. You can't say you're surprised, all things considered!'

'I, you, they, it, can't...'

'Do you want me to come back when you're a little more awake?'

'Well, could you?' Kimberley felt ridiculous and was grateful for the darkness when John replied.

'Let me just see what space I've got in my diary for mental connections with curious psychology students.' There was an awkward silence for a moment and she imagined John flicking the pages of some invisible diary. 'Nope, shouldn't be a problem.

Except the fact I don't get to choose when I can do this. So now is probably the best time.'

'Where are you?'

'In solitary. The Warden was mildly upset with my performance, apparently.'

'But how are you talking to me, then?'

Moving along the window, Kimberley kept her back pressed against the cold glass. Reaching the wall, her fingers fumbled for the light switch.

'I'd prefer you didn't turn the light on.' It was too late. No sooner had he spoken, the apartment was bathed in bright light.

'Stop messing around. How did you escape?'

'I told you, I'm still in solitary. Deep in the bowels of this awful place.' John sighed as Kimberley scanned the room for any sign of him. 'You'll do well to find me in there.'

'How are you talking to me then?' Pinching herself, hoping she would suddenly wake up.

'Whatever connection we had from those memories has lingered. It's not something I'm used to, not something I've tried on my own and I don't know how long it will last, so we should be quick.'

'What do you want from me?'

Kimberley moved around the room, checking every recess and corner as John spoke, but his voice seemed to be coming from everywhere and yet nowhere. Checking the front door was still locked, she turned back and faced into the room, seeing her reflection in the glass of the expansive window. Still dressed in the same clothes, her hair was a mess and she realised she looked as bad as she felt. Pushing the thoughts aside, Kimberley focussed her attention on John's voice.

'I need you to come back tomorrow, ask to see me again.'

'Why would I do that?'

'Because of what you've seen.' John's voice was calm, his words sounding almost inviting. 'You can;t say I haven't tickled your curiosity.'

'Whatever you did to me, I don't want any part of it again.'

'It's too late for that.' He corrected. 'I could see the curiosity in your eyes, the fact you fought with the idea you may believe me. That's why I took the chance to let you in.'

'And what if I didn't want to go in there? What if I didn't want to see any of that?'

'It's a little too late for that. And now you have been there, I need you to come back.'

'I don't want to see that again. I don't want to see that monster, that thing, ever again.'

Kimberley's eyes fell on the pad that had fallen to the floor and the crude sketch of the Ripper she had made. More than anything, she had focussed on the lifeless eyes and imposing figure that had moved like a living shadow before taking shape before her eyes. Even the memory sent a shudder down her spine, and she quickly ripped her attention away from the notepad.

'I said the same.' John's voice crackled as he spoke, as if there was interference affecting him. 'You left your paperwork behind and something there caused me great concern.'

'Your own file?'

'No, a newspaper cutting you had amongst the papers. I'm not sure what it had to do with why you came to the hospital, but I need to know more.'

The voice was fading, growing more distant as John continued to speak.

'I can't come back. Running away like that, I expect the warden has already spoken to the university.'

'You can try.' John's voice was barely above a whisper now. 'Please.'

'I'll do what I can.' Kimberley offered, but she got no reply. 'Are you still there?'

Unnerved by the feeling she was alone and somehow not, Kimberley remained against the door for some time before she dared to make her way back across to the chair by the window. Looking down at the pad, she picked it up and folded the pages over, once again hiding the crude drawing of the Ripper's silhouette. The topmost page was adorned with words and the image of the Raven's curious appearance.

Tracing her fingers across the hooked nose of the Raven's plague doctor mask, she realised how odd the whole appearance was. Somehow his clothing was already at odds with the Gothic Victorian surroundings and yet she couldn't picture a period in time where he would have fitted. It was as if someone had somehow plucked him from an alternative place, existing alongside the one he had been in before, and brought into this world.

'Oh, stop being so stupid.' Kimberley scorned herself and tossed the notepad down onto the chair. 'It's all just a bloody dream.'

Turning away from the panoramic window, Kimberley made her way up the narrow flight of steps leading up to the raised bedroom in the open-plan apartment. Throwing herself down on the bed, she spent a long time staring up at the ceiling before sleep once again took hold. Unlike before, her sleep was dreamless and most importantly, silent.

7

AGAINST BETTER JUDGEMENT

Morning broke, and even as she ate her breakfast, Kimberley had not made up her mind. Her sleep had been uneasy, and she had seen almost every hour pass by through the night until the dawn sunlight poured in through the window. Showering after her breakfast, she soon emerged from the bathroom and once again approached the expansive window. Painted in the warm morning glow of the sun, the city looked nothing like it had in the misty night air when she had arrived home. London had been her home for some years now, forsaking her rural roots to chase her research. She had always been on the move, yet this apartment was the longest she had stayed in one place over the last nine years.

Unplugging her phone from the kitchen worktop, she moved to rest against the back of the seat in front of the window. Knowing nobody could see her, dressed only in her dressing gown, she rested her elbows on the soft material and took a moment to think things through. All the while, she kept her attention out of the window, making sure her gaze did not drift to the notepad.

Mulling over all the possibilities, her fingers unlocked the phone, and she quickly scanned through her contacts until she found the one she wanted. Pausing for a moment, she made her decision and hit the *dial* button and put the phone onto speaker. In a matter of seconds, the phone was ringing and after a half-dozen rings, a familiar voice answered the call.

'Miss Mansfield, I must say I'm surprised.'

'Warden.' Kimberley offered, blushing despite being alone in her apartment. 'I need to apologise for yesterday. It wasn't very professional and...'

'You're right, I would have expected such childish behaviour from a first-year student. Not one from someone with your level of experience.' Kimberley felt uncomfortable and knew this call was as much about damage control as it was about finding out what had happened the day before.

Deep down, Kimberley knew the damage such a foolish reaction could have. Not only in her career, but in her position and research. Having decided to contact the warden, she was doing it more out of self-preservation than to appease John, but deep down she had an insatiable curiosity about what had happened.

'That patient, John, he just unnerved me. It's not something I'm used to doing, I've never reacted that way before.'

'I know.' The warden's harsh voice interjected. 'I've spoken with your professor and your behaviour quite astounded him.'

Knowing she was definitely on dangerous ground, Kimberley was quick to allay any concern from the warden. Having only spoken to the woman via conference calls, never having met her in person, she was familiar with the warden's stern nature.

'I would like to pick up where I left off, if you'd be willing to give me a second chance?'

Leaving the question unanswered for an uncomfortable amount of time, Kimberley knew the warden was toying with her. In all of their correspondence leading up to her arriving at the Nuthall Hospital, she had picked up on the warden's need to assert her authority. Ever the playful hunter, Kimberley had met her fair share of people in similar positions and knew the personalities that came with the territory. Even her professor, a timid and quiet man, had warned her about the types of people who found their lives surrounded by delicate minds.

'I don't think a second visit with Mr Smith would be advisable.'

'On the contrary,' Kimberley quickly interrupted. 'I'd like to finish what I started with him. I think he was starting to open up to me.'

'A man like John Smith is nothing but a manipulator. Giving you access to him was a mistake, and not one I am keen to make again.'

Kimberley weighed up her options on how to tackle the tensions between them. Appreciating the warden's temperament, she knew the woman was testing her.

'If I'm not mistaken, the agreement between the university and the hospital gave me access to any prisoners who were category matches for my research. John Smith is one of those candidates and I'm sure the ethics committee wouldn't be too happy if I had to change venues at the last minute.'

'A change brought about by your childishness.' The warden snapped back.

Kimberley let her warning linger for a moment, knowing the warden would be seething at the sudden change of tact from her. That said, she also knew it was a calculated risk that had the potential to appeal to the warden's nature. After what felt like an age, the warden offered a curt and simple answer to her threat.

'John will be ready for you in an hour. I suggest you get moving. I've already affected the daily routine of my patients.'

The call ended abruptly, and Kimberley dropped it down onto the seat in front of her. Sighing to herself, she buried her head into her arms and took a few moments to compose herself before making her move to get dressed and head out to the hospital.

***

By the time Kimberley had navigated the morning rush hour and arrived at the grand gates of the Nuthall Hospitals, she had convinced herself the warden would not be there to greet her.

Walking to the gates, she pressed the call button on the post beside the gates and waited for it to ring.

'Welcome back.' The familiar gruff voice of the orderly crackled over the speaker. 'Use the side gate.'

Hearing the lock open, Kimberley pushed on the pedestrian gate and made sure it was secured behind her. Knowing she was being watched by the cameras mounted on every face of the hospital walls, Kimberley took a deep breath in and walked towards the expansive steps leading to the main doors. Climbing the sweeping stairs, she reached the door and stepped into the familiar reception of the hospital.

'The warden has asked me to escort you down.' The orderly announced through the speaker as Kimberley emptied her pockets into a plastic tray and placed it on the conveyor belt.

'Will I be able to speak with her?' Kimberley pressed as she stepped into the airlock scanner.

'I doubt it. I'm not sure she's in the mood, all things considered.'

Waiting for the door to open, Kimberley felt all eyes on her as the scanner made its slow pass over her body. Once the scan was complete, the glass door rotated open, and she stepped out to retrieve her belongings.

'Where are the papers I left behind yesterday?' Kimberley asked as she scooped her belongings and quickly followed behind the orderly who had already set off.

'They're waiting for you in the interview room.'

'Can I ask something?'

'You're the type who would ask, even if I said no.'

The orderly's less than welcoming manner caught her by surprise. Although she had known that her challenge of the warden's authority would have left her isolated from the stern woman, she had not expected it to resonate with the staff. Not wanting to appear unphased by the cold answers, Kimberley pressed as she followed along the winding corridors and into the elevator overlooking *The Deck*.

'How long has John been here?'

'What does it say in his file?'

'Were you here when he arrived?'

'He was a patient when I started. I've only been here for six, no, seven years.' The orderly offered as they reached the ground floor and the doors opened. 'John hasn't been in the general population at all since I arrived.'

'Why's that?'

'He has a way of upsetting people.' The orderly unlocked the doors to the older wing. 'As you learned yesterday.'

'Has he done that to other people too, then?'

'How other patients react to one another isn't really an easy way to assess how they affect people. Damaged minds affected by other damaged minds is hardly a stable assessment.'

'Why wasn't that in his files?'

'There's a lot that won't be held in the files the warden has shared with you.' The orderly stopped at the same interview cell she had been in the day before. 'That's your job now. To fill in the gaps by talking to him.'

'Are you going to be watching again?' Kimberley pressed as he unlocked the door.

'What? In case you decide to run out again?' Offering her a knowing smirk, he pulled the door open and stepped aside. 'If you could gather your paperwork up before you run away this time, please.'

Doing her best not to bite at the orderly's jibes, she offered him a dismissive glare and stepped into the room. As soon as she had passed over the threshold, the door slammed shut behind her and she focussed her attention on John. Bruises showing on his face, he offered her a wry smile as she drank in his battered appearance.

'What did they do to you?'

'Oh, what, these?' John chuckled and moved his hands in front of his face.

In the split second, his hands had covered his face, the bruises had disappeared and he once again looked fresher faced and playful. Offer her a coy wink. He motioned for her to take a seat on the other side of the table. Unlike before, his hands were shackled tighter, his movements were restricted, and he could barely reach to touch the table.

'How did you do that?'

'Parlour tricks. It gives the bully boys out there some reward for their brutish behaviour.' John quipped. 'Besides, I can hardly bruise when my icy heart hasn't beat in over a hundred years now, can I?'

'About that.'

'Please don't say you're going to sit there and pretend it wasn't real.'

'It's just, well, you know?'

'Please, can we accept the fact I shared a more than intimate memory with you? And, not to mention, spoke to you while you were in bed.'

'So it was you and not just some dream?' Despite the question, Kimberley had known it was John and was not a figment of a cloudy imagination.

Rising an eyebrow, John stared at her across the table. For the longest time, his hands in the smaller cuffs that help them almost palm to palm. 'Anyway, I've got questions about that news headline.'

'What about it?' Kimberley peered over the table but refused to reach for the cutting. 'It's just something I was considering looking into.'

'Pretty convenient, wouldn't you say?'

'How so?'

'After what you saw yesterday, I'm sure you can see why the headline piqued my attention.'

'It's just a glorifying headline, designed to sell more newspapers.'

'What about the crimes? Do they match the Ripper I showed you?' John's playful nature had evaporated and for a moment, Kimberley saw the intensity in his face she had seen when he had been resurrected as the Raven.

'I don't know too much about it.'

'You're lying.'

'I beg your pardon,' Kimberley stammered as her gaze shifted to the camera in the corner of the room.

'I can see it in your eyes. When you've been around as long as I have, you get a sense for these things. So please, don't insult me.'

'I'm sorry. I only know what's been reported in the news.'

'And?'

'They're saying it's a copycat of Jack The Ripper. Yes, their crimes are similar.'

'In which case, my hibernation in here is over.' John locked gazes with her and said his next words with great care, except his lips didn't move and she heard only his voice in her head. 'I need you to help me escape.'

'Not a chance.

'Keep calm.' Still, John's lips did not move. 'I won't ask anything more from you than to release me from these restraints. We will do the rest.'

'I'm not sure I can do that.' Kimberley was trembling as she spoke, her voice hushed to avoid the orderly hearing what she was saying. 'It would cost me my career.'

'I'll make it look like you weren't involved. You saw what that thing did in London.'

'I thought you killed it.' Kimberley protested.

'Clearly not.' John held out his hands towards her. 'Now please, you know what we have to do.'

Unsure of what to do, Kimberley perched uneasily on the edge of her seat. Knowing the eyes of the orderly, and most likely the warden, were transfixed on the camera feed from the room, she didn't know what she could do.

'Please.' John pressed, this time his lips moving with the words he spoke.

8

— ∘ —

THE RAVEN

The aged Victorian wing of the Nuthall Hospital was eerily quiet. Within the corridor outside the interview cell, it was devoid of staff or any signs of life. The orderly observation station was along the length of the brick-lined passage and out of the way. Unloved and somewhat left on a slow journey to decay, it seemed fitting they had left John and a select few other inmates in that part of the building. Despite its age, the facilities were still secure and relied less on technology and more on the brutish security of brick and steel.

Despite the eerie silence, the door of the interview cell shuddered on its hinges. As dust fell from the brickwork, the orderly burst into the corridor from the observation room and looked towards the secured door. Again, the door shuddered, and the orderly launched along the corridor in response. As he reached the door, the metal frame exploded out of the wall, sending him crashing back into a cloud of dust and debris.

As the dust dissipated, the dazed man brushed off the mortar that had landed on his torso and stared wide-eyed as a silhouetted figure emerged through the jagged opening. At first the shape appeared distorted, somehow human, and yet not. What emerged from the cloud of billowing dust was not a man, it was the figure of a man, it was *The Raven*.

Once again, wearing the long black coat and plague doctor mask, John emerged through the dust and dominated the corridor.

'What the hell are you?' The orderly stammered as he scrambled on all fours through the debris.

'Sometimes the most unbelievable stories are true.' John declared, his voice muffled by the mask. 'Maybe next time you should take a moment to consider the truth behind the madness.'

'Smith?'

'No. The Raven.'

Turning his back on the orderly, his coat billowed behind him dramatically. Taking two steps, he heard the racking of the extendable baton and turned to look back at the young man. Unable to show his expression, John tilted his head to one side curiously and waited for the inevitable attack. Raising the baton, the orderly was fighting against the surge of fear as the metal weapon shook in his hand.

'You're not going anywhere.'

'I wouldn't waste your time.' John dismissed and turned away.

The attack came and, much to the orderly's dismay, the racked baton collided with the Raven's back and stopped dead in its tracks. Unflinching, he rotated on the spot and grabbed the metal bar, pulling the orderly closer. Only able to see his own reflecting in the large lenses of the mask's eyes, the orderly fumbled with his words as the Raven looked down at him.

'You...you...'

'Don't waste your breath.' John landed a solid blow on the other man's temple and allowed his unconscious body to slump to the ground. 'You don't know how long I've waited to do that.'

Discarding the now bent baton, John stalked along the corridor, leaving the unconscious orderly and a stunned Kimberley in his wake. Bursting through the doors into the new wing and out into *The Deck*, the sudden harsh light caught him by surprise. Emerging into the vast open space, he made it halfway towards the glass lift shaft before the air was filled with the sound of a blaring siren.

'Whatever this theatrical display is about, it ends now.' The warden's voice echoed in the vast space from the speakers mounted on the walls. 'I thought we were past all this, John.'

'It's time for me to leave.' John declared to the open air. 'I'd appreciate you making that as easy as possible.'

'We both know that's not going to happen.'

Standing in the middle of the room, he realised someone had already secured away the other inmates in their rooms. Turning around, the sound of speedy footfalls stole his attention from behind an imposing set of secured doors. Bracing himself, John cast his glance skyward and towards the skylight high above.

After a few long seconds, the doors burst open and a dozen armour-clad men marched in file into the room.

Dressed in blue coveralls and armoured in public order padding, they looked like police officers preparing for a riot. Fanning out, they formed into an extended line behind a barrier of transparent shields. Stretching the width of the room, they formed a solid barrier between John and his route out of the hospital. Rattling their batons on the front of the shields, the room became a cacophony of pounding as a half-dozen armed men took positions behind the shields.

Armed with stun guns and pistols, John knew he was in for a fight. The fact he had been hiding in the withering shell of his human form, the sudden opportunity to reconnect with his powers sent a buzz of excitement coursing through him.

'You don't want to do this.' John warned as he shrugged off the heavy black coat and removed the pair of escrima sticks from his back.

Testing the weight of his familiar weapons, John dropped into a defensive stance and prepared himself for the fight. In unison, the line of shields marched towards him. Biding his time, John watched the space between them close, all the while watching the wandering armed guards behind the line of shields. When the first shield got within striking distance, John made his move.

Dropping his weight into his legs, John launched up into the air and dived over the line of shields to land on the sterile floor behind the advancing line. Reacting as quickly as they could beneath their protective clothing, John disarmed the two nearest guards and sending them flying across the room. Making quick work of two more, the air was filled with the *crackle* of electricity as one of the armed guards fired their stun gun.

Feeling the barbs bite into his skin, John's body immediately locked up, and he fell to the ground writhing as the circuit sent his muscles into contraction.

'Get on him.' One of the guards screamed.

Feeling the weight of bodies diving on top of him, John was powerless against the waves of electricity immobilising him. Losing any view of the room beneath the sea of armour-clad bodies, John felt the relentless impact of blows as the guards set about doing their best to restrain him.

'I've got his hands.' Another voice screamed in panic.

'Get the cuffs.'

Mind racing, knowing if they succeeded in restraining him, his escape attempt would be over. John tried to calm his screaming mind but the flurry of confusion from his spasming muscles filled his brain.

'Move out of the way.'

As one of the guards adjusted their position to give them access to handcuff John, they managed to disconnect one of the probes from his leg and, in an instant, all sensation returned to his body. Not wasting time to celebrate the sudden return of his senses, John took full advantage of the change in circumstances. Finding footing, John pushed up and broke free from the heavy weight of the guards piling on top of him.

Sending bodies flying in all directions, John took a deep breath and watched as the world moved in slow motion around him. To him, the world moved in slow motion while to the world he moved with impossible speed. Ducking beneath a laboured punch thrown by the nearest guard, John delivered a solid upper-cut to the man's chin, lifting him into the air and ripping the Nato helmet from his head.

Moving to his next victim, John disarmed the man, ripping the self-loading pistol from his grasp as a round exploded from the short muzzle. Ignoring the projectile, John slammed his elbow into the next guarding sending a spider-web of cracks across the helmet visor. Moving along the line, John dispatched five of the guards before the disregarded bullet sank into his shoulder.

As the round bit into his skin, his momentum was lost and everything once again moved at normal speed. The five guards he had dealt with were now out of the equation and, to his dismay, the nearest two were armed with pistols. Firing a handful of rounds, John felt each of them find their mark in different parts of his body. Being dead had its advantages. Despite ripping through his torso and organs, the bullets could do no damage. Being nothing more than a distracting inconvenience that had halted his speedy attacks, John backed away until the two guards' magazines were empty.

'Waste of bullets, wouldn't you say?' John jibed as he admired the holes in his clothes.

As the guards instinctively reloaded, John attacked and immediately disarmed them. Snatching the top-slide from both weapons, both men looked on in horror as John grabbed the closest of the two and launched up into the air towards the enormous skylight high above. Crashing through the glass, the guard shrieked in terror as the remaining armed guards opened fire and John landed on the other side of the shattered reinforced glass.

Wind whipping around them, John span around and held the guard over the hole he had created in the glass. With the guard in the way, the firing from below stopped and John was able to speak with his hostage.

'What are you?' The guard stammered as John pulled the helmet off the man's head.

The guard was only in his early twenties and despite everything, John felt a wave of guilt at the terror on the young man's face. Taking a moment, John removed the plague doctor mask from his head and felt the cool breeze on his face.

'I'm the thing you've ignored and kept locked in the basement for too long.' John took a moment to savour the chilled air and the impressive view of London from atop the hospital building. 'I am Death's hand.'

'Don't kill me.' The young guard pleaded, balancing precariously on the shattered glass.

'Kill you?' John smirked. 'I'm here to protect you. Well, until Death requires your attention.'

'When's that going to be?'

'Not today!' John hushed and dropped the guard to the side of the gaping hole in the skylight.

Leaving the cowering man on the roof, John sauntered to the edge of the roof and looked down at the city below. It had been a while and yet the familiarity of the capital was still there. Searching the skyline, John saw Tower Bridge in the distance and a wry smile appeared on his face as he replaced the plague doctor mask on his head. Securing the leather straps in place, John turned his head to the sun and drank in his newfound freedom.

'Are you even with me these days?' John asked the empty space to his side.

Getting no answer, not honestly expecting one, John balanced on the edge of the roof. Hearing nothing but the roar of traffic below, John turned back to face the guard, who was delicately crawling away from the jagged hole in the skylight.

'Where are you going to go?' The man hollered as he clambered to safety.

'Back to my perch, watching over you all.'

As he finished his declaration, John leaned back, flipped into the air and over the edge of the roof. Allowing gravity to take its hold on him, John tumbled towards the ground and revelled in the excitement he had not felt in a long time.

By the time the guard reached the precarious ledge, there was no sign of John anywhere to be seen. Rolling onto his back, the guard stared up towards the moody clouds and allowed the tears of fear to roll down his cheeks.

What John left behind was a stark warning that he had been caged for too long. A fact he was not prepared to let happen again.

The Raven was once again free to honour his oath.

9

— · —

IN THE WAKE OF DAMAGE

Kimberley emerged from the cell after the sirens had stopped. Tentatively making her way back towards *The Deck*, she gasped at the sight that greeted her.

Bruised and battered, the armour-clad guards were in the process of collecting up the broken and discarded equipment. Catching the gaze of a bloodied guard whose helmet hung cracked on his belt, the man glared at her with contempt. The right side of his face was already swollen, the bruising showing across his cheek and eye-socket.

'Miss Mansfield.' The familiarity of the warden's voice sent a chill down her spine.

Looking around, Kimberley caught sight of the suited warden standing on the far side of the room. Hair swept back in a tight ponytail, her tailored grey suit added to the coldness she had become accustomed too. Following the warden's gaze, Kimberley couldn't help but gasp again as she saw the jagged hole in the glass skylight many levels above them.

'How did that happen?' Kimberley hushed as she made her way through the flow of recovering guards.

'I would expect you are well aware of how.' The warden snapped back, dismissing one of the guards from her side. 'Care to explain how my patient has escaped and you seem untouched, and unphased, by it all?'

Knowing the warden's suspicions would be levelled at her, Kimberley steeled herself as she made her way to stand in front of the middle-aged woman. Holding the warden's gaze, Kimberley suppressed the nervousness that coursed through her and waited for the inevitable interrogation that would follow.

'I don't know what happened,' She lied. 'One minute we were sat talking, and the next, he...changed.'

'Changed?'

'It's hard to explain.'

'Try.'

Knowing the truth about what had happened, Kimberley was able to sell her disbelief with absolute confidence. Having been seated across from John, the moment he had become the Raven had been a truly terrifying sight to behold. Seated across from him at the table, John had done nothing more than close his eyes and uttered a handful of words she could not make out. Whatever language they were spoken in, they were like nothing she had heard before. As he had finished speaking, Kimberley had watched the plague mask grow over his face, as if it had been there all along and somehow been invisible.

Rising from the table as the flowing black coat had materialised over his body, the chains of his restraints had fallen to the floor. Once everything had changed about his outward appearance, he had placed both hands on the table and leaned across the gap between them. His muffled words still echoed in her mind as she replayed the events in her memory.

'You'd do well to step aside. I have no intention of hurting you. In fact, I'd quite like to see you again.'

As soon as he she had moved aside, John, the Raven, had moved to the door and made his dramatic escape. Casting one last look back at her as the billowing dust exploded around him, Kimberley knew beneath the leather and metal mask he was smiling.

'Well?' The warden interrupted, snatching her back from her memory. 'What can you tell me?'

'The man that left that room was not John Smith. The man that left that room, well, I don't think it was a man.'

'You have been nothing but a problem. Come with me.' The warden snapped as she turned on her heels and stalked towards the open lift doors.

'This wasn't my fault.' Kimberley protested as she followed behind the warden.

Stepping into the lift, the older woman slammed a clenched fist into the control panel and waited for the doors to close as Kimberley fidgeted by her side. Once the doors had closed, the warden turned on Kimberley and towered over her, pressing her back into the corner of the lift. Terrified by the sudden coldness and aggression, Kimberley tried not to shake as the lift climb upwards and the older woman glared down at her.

'In twenty-four hours, you've set my team back in John's treatment program. What's more than that is the fact you've allowed him to escape.'

'I didn't allow anything.' Kimberley defended but fell silent from adding anything further.

'Whatever you did, and I know you did something, it has cost the reputation of my establishment. That is something that I cannot and will not accept.' The lift took an age to reach the upper levels and Kimberley felt relief as it ground to a halt. 'You'll forgive me if I rescind your open invitation to return for your research.'

Snatching the visitor label from her top, the warden snapped the printed plastic and allowed it to drop to the floor. Moving aside, she beckoned for Kimberley to leave the lift and rather than argue, Kimberley stepped out into the corridor in silence. With the warden stalking behind her, she guided Kimberley through the corridors and to a large room she had never been to before.

Reaching an imposing frosted-glass door, the warden barged past and thrust open the door before stepping into her modern office. Motioning with her hand for Kimberley to follow her, she moved to her seat behind a large black oak table and dropped down into it. Resting her elbows on the table, her demeanour changed as she rested her head in both hands and let out a long sigh.

'I'm sorry.' The warden eventually conceded as she pointed for Kimberley to sit. 'I know this isn't your fault. You have to understand the inquiries that will follow. It's just, I've spent my whole career building order from chaos and in a single day it's all come crashing down.'

There was sadness in her voice as she spoke, and Kimberley couldn't help but feel a sense of guilt. The stern warden had, in the matter of a few seconds, changed from the imposing figure to something akin to a broken woman. Sensing it was the fact they were no longer under the scrutiny of her employees, Kimberley sat quietly and waited to see what would happen.

'You'll need to be part of the investigation into how this happened,' The warden explained as she leaned back in the luxurious seat, her expression somewhat softer now. 'I don't expect it will be a speedy process.'

'I'll help in any way I can.'

'I know you will.'

'What will happen now?' Kimberley quizzed, as the warden reached for a crystal decanter from beside the desk and poured herself a long draw of whiskey.

'I've already reported the escape to the board. They've advised we are best dealing with it internally.'

'Hold on, don't the authorities need alerting?'

'As I explained before. We aren't behest of the national health service, we are equal parts private, and public funded. It gives us autonomy over internal matters.'

'So who will investigate any of this?'

'The board have their own processes.'

'Sounds a bit questionable.'

'Don't confuse my concern for weakness.' The warden interjected, catching herself before reverting to her aggressive and dominating nature. 'We will compile the necessary reports for the authorities, but we will keep this matter contained. At the request of the governing bodies.'

'And who exactly are they, the governing body?'

Feeling the warden's gaze on her, Kimberley looked around the room and admired the plethora of certificates and qualifications lining the walls. A large painting dominated the wall behind the desk, an abstract picture that appeared to show a crescent moon rising at an awkward angle. Sensing the warden's attention on her, Kimberley lowered her gaze and watched the woman take a long sip from her glass.

'It's probably better I don't prepare you for any questions. It would hardly be impartial if you knew everything about the function and workings of my hospital.'

'Agreed.' Kimberley conceded, not in any way believing what she was saying. 'So when does this all begin?'

'Our priority will be locating and apprehending John Smith. The investigation team will be supplementary to that.'

'So, what am I supposed to do?'

'We will be in touch.'

Leaving Kimberley hanging, the warden did nothing to dismiss her. Instead, she simply turned her chair around and faced the strange painting on the wall. Not wanting to overstay her welcome, Kimberley rose from the chair and moved towards the door.

'By the way.' The warden offered with a wave of her hand, still keeping the chair facing away. 'I will have your paperwork delivered to you, once we've gone through the contents. As part of the investigation of course.'

'Whatever you like.' Kimberley huffed and yanked the door open.

Navigating the interior of the hospital, Kimberley passed through the security gates and emerged into the early afternoon sun. Taking a moment at the top of the steps to the hospital, she couldn't help shake the feeling she was being watched. Turning her attention to the vast pale frontage, she caught sight of the warden standing by the glass of her office window looking down at her. Feeling the older woman's steely gaze, Kimberley pulled her coat tighter around her and hastily descended the sweeping steps.

Only when she was far from the Nuthall Hospital did she find a place to stop. Finding herself in a small public park, Kimberley found an empty bench and dropped down heavily onto the damp wood. As soon as she sat, she allowed herself to show her true feelings about what had just happened.

Having fought to suppress her fear and emotion, Kimberley had worn her mask of confidence as best she could. Fighting to keep the tremble from her hands, she had been relieved when the warden had dismissed her. Knowing full well the woman would not trust a word she was saying, Kimberley had made sure she was alone before allowing her a moment of release.

As tears streamed down her face, Kimberley looked at her shaking hands and felt a sense of dread and fear as she turned her gaze up towards the moody sky.

'What have I done?' Kimberley sobbed as she sat back on the bench, allowing her head to roll back. 'How could I have been so bloody stupid?'

Kimberley remained on the bench for some time before she felt the soft patter of raindrops on her face. Forcing herself to move, Kimberley gathered herself together and made her way back to her apartment. Moving through the growing crowds of shoppers, tourists and workers, she was grateful for the anonymity the busy city gave her. Despite seeing nothing, Kimberley was sure she was being followed but by the time she reached her station on the underground, she no longer had the inclination or energy to take a longer or more convoluted route to show out anyone who might be following her.

Knowing, if the warden had sent them, they would know her home address she decided the safest option was to go about her business. Acting in any other way would risk making her look suspicious. Opting for the safest course of action, Kimberley returned home and was relieved to lock the door and secure it from the inside.

Turning away from the door, Kimberley leaned against it and slowly slid down to sit on the carpeted floor. Looking across the open-plan apartment, she was about to move when a sudden voice spoke from the far corner of the room.

'I thought you'd never come home.'

Appearing from behind the dividing wall between the elevated bedroom and the rest of the apartment, Kimberley gasped as John leaned against the low wall. Still wearing the long black coat, he removed the plague doctor mask from his face and offered her a wry smile as he looked down at her.

'How the hell did you get in here?'

'Is that all you can think to ask?'

'Get out.' Kimberley boomed as she stood up. 'If they catch you here, I'm done for. I've done my part, now please leave.'

In the blink of an eye, John disappeared from the bedroom space and reappeared standing in front of Kimberley. Gasping at the sudden teleportation, Kimberley backed against the door and stared wide-eyed at John.

'How?'

'Shall we talk, or should I just leave?'

Kimberley ripped the door open and step aside, giving John a clear path into the hallway.

'You can leave.' She didn't meet his gaze but her voice was firm.

Taking his leave, John walked past her and offered one last hushed comment as he brushed past her.

'You're already involved, more than you know. You'll know where to find me, when you change your mind.'

10

— : —

A FAMILIAR CRIME SCENE

London looked different than John remembered. In the thirty years since he had arrived at the Nuthall Hospital, a lot had changed, not least of all the people that meandered the busy streets. Needing to be away from the crowds, John now found himself perched on the edge of Nelson's Column overlooking Trafalgar Square. Silhouetted by the bright exterior of the National Gallery, he remained obscured by the shadows created by the spotlights directed at the infamous statue behind him.

In his guise as The Raven, John was able to remain hidden from view and had watched the dying sun set behind the skyline of impressive buildings. Surrounded by the more traditional London buildings he remembered from his past, John somehow felt more at home here than he did amongst the crowds below. Watching the evening play out, John remained perched on the edge of the marble platform until the moon had risen high into the night sky.

'Not what it used to be, wouldn't you say?'

Once again John looked around, somehow hoping that Death would answer him from the heavy shadows cast by Nelson's statue. Getting no reply, John removed the mask from his face and admired it in the moonlight. Having been unable to manifest himself as The Raven, it had been a long time since he had admired the intricate design of the leather mask.

Tracing his fingers around the shimmering lenses, he brought the mask closer to admire the fine embossed detailing that covered each face of the plague doctor mask. moving along the length of the curved nose, his fingers reached the metal embossed tip of the beak and he felt the cold metal against his fingertips.

'How long has it been since I wore this?' He quizzed himself as he turned over the mask. 'It still feels the same when it's on my face.'

Bringing the mask closer, John was about to the replace it on his face but stopped short as the moonlight caught the inside of the plague mask. Something caught his eye that he had not noticed before. Rising to his feet, he moved around the platform until he was bathed in the bright light of the spotlights mounted at the base of the statue.

'An oath. An honour. Death's hand in human form.' John read aloud the sentences etched into the metal rim of the right lens.

In all the years wearing the mask, he had never noticed the lettering and had a sneaking suspicion it had not always been there. Inspecting the inside of the mask for anything else he had not noticed before, he found nothing. Feeling the frustration building inside him, John once again looked beyond the statue and the silhouetted skyline of buildings that surrounded him.

'Death's hand. So where the hell are you?'

Scrunching the leather mask in his hand, John stepped to the edge and allowed the mask to fall from his grip. Tumbling to the ground far below, John watched until he could no longer see it falling. Lifting his attention from the people below, John knew he needed a purpose, knew he needed to find the reason he had felt the desire to leave the confines of the hospital. Despite having found peace within the confines of the walls, there had always been something itching inside him and having seen the newspaper clipping, John knew it had something to do with the headline.

Once again removing the crumpled paper from his pocket, John read the headline and the article once again. All the while, his attention was drawn to the word **RIPPER** that seemed to almost call to him from the page. While Kimberley had dismissed the article as a typical sensationalist headliner, there was something in his instincts that told John this was something more.

'Fine!' John huffed as he replaced the cutting in his pocket. 'If I'm ever going to get some peace, I need to see what this has to do with me.'

Looking down at the ground far below, John offered a wry smile and took his leap of faith out into the air.

Seated on the raised plinth of the infamous column, two young students sat drinking and talking. Oblivious to all that was happening above them, they had not noticed the discarded plague doctor mask tumble to the ground behind them. Engrossed in their conversation, neither had any awareness of what was happening until John crashed into the stone platform right behind them.

Landing with a sickening *crunch*, both of them screamed as John's lifeless body came to rest at an awkward angle on the pale stone. Confused by what had happened, the two strangers backed away from John's body, wide-eyed and stammering to find their words.

'How'd he get there?' One of them eventually mustered.

'Must have jumped.'

'What, from up there?'

'We should check if he's alive.'

'Go on then, you check him.' Pushing his friend forward, the other was caught by surprise and offered a scowl.

Inching closer, the young man looked down at John's face and the fact his eyes were still open. Leaning closer, he held a shaking hand over John's mouth and felt no warm breath against his skin.

'Damn, I think he's dead.'

'Is there any blood?'

Dropping to his knees, the man reached out to check beneath John's head for any blood when the impossible happened. As his fingertips brushed John's hair, he turned to look at the man leaning over him.

'As nice as that may be, mind if I get up?' Knowing terror would freeze the man, John couldn't help but smile as he sat up.

Unable to move, the young man's mouth opened and closed as he fought to find his voice to scream. Cracking his neck and shoulders, John felt his bones return to their proper positions. When his body had recovered from the sudden impact, John rose to his feet and looked down at the young man who remained on his knees with his mouth opening and closing comically.

'Could you pass me that?' John asked as he straightened the collar of his coat, pointing out the discarded mask by the kneeling man's side. 'Probably shouldn't have let it go like that.'

Dumbfounded by what was happening, the young man picked up the mask and help it up for John to take. Offering a courteous smile, John took it and replaced it on his head. Once the leather straps were secured, he pulled up the hood of his coat and took a moment to compose himself. Knowing he was still finding his connection to the powers Death had given him, he was in a delicate transition back to himself.

'You'd do well not to tell anyone about any of this.' he offered, his voice muffled by the mask. 'I can't imagine people would believe it and, trust me, you don't want to look like you belong in a mental hospital.'

Before either of the young man could reply, John launched himself off the stone base and disappeared into the night. Leaving both of them dumbstruck by what had just happened. How a man had crashed into the stone base and simply brushed it off, was beyond comprehension.

Wasting no time in the fact he had found enough connection to his powers, John moved through the London streets like a spectre in the night. Unseen by anyone, he moved at an impossible speed through the streets, leaving nothing behind but a dark vapour trail along the path he had come. Having stalked the shadows of London for decades, John knew exactly where he needed to go and how he was going to get there.

In a matter of seconds, he had made it halfway across the capital and allowed his journey to end as he entered Whitechapel.

Allowing his racing senses to settle, John realised he was in Buck's Row, but the street sign now read Durward Street. Taking in his surroundings, John realised how much had changed and yet he sensed the familiarity of his newfound surroundings. Turning in the middle of the cobbled street, John's attention was drawn to the flashing blue lights of a police van and solitary officer in a high-visibility jacket at the far end of the road.

Removing the mask and allowing his appearance to change and match his surroundings, John approached the tired constable that leant against the bonnet of the idling van.

'Can't go down this way, mate.' The grumpy officer waved as John approached.

'What's happened here?'

'You kidding? Been all over the news.' The young policeman muttered. 'You ain't some reporter, are you?'

'No, I've been away for a while.'

Thrusting a leaflet into John's hand, the policeman turned away and opened the door to sit inside the police van. Turning away from the secured crime scene, John read the information leaflet the officer had given him. John's heart sank as he read through the warning leaflet that detailed the fact police had discovered a young woman's body in the early hours of the morning and were appealing for witnesses. Sensing death in the air, John ensured he was out of the police officer's view before he once again became The Raven and transported himself into the alley beyond the crime scene tape that fluttered in the gentle breeze.

Stepping into the shadows of the alleyway, John looked around and felt his heart sink as he saw the splatters of blood that had sprayed across the brickwork. Relieved to see they had removed the body, there were enough indications of where the young woman had died to draw him to the right place. Closing his eyes, John felt his mind wander back into what had happened in the dreary alleyway.

In his mind, he saw the victim, a young woman no older than Kimberley, entering the alley and finding her way blocked by an imposing figure at the far end. Silhouetted by the streetlight, the enormous figure stepped into the flickering light and John ripped his eyes open and turned to face where the figure had been.

'It can't be.' John gasped as he realised the figure that had blocked the alley was none other than the Ripper.

Needing to escape the confines of the alleyway, John burst from the shadows and ran through the fluttering of police tape to the surprise of the officer in the van. Unable to react, the policeman screamed after him as John disappeared into the anonymity of the night.

Having escaped knowing something was unbalanced in the world, John had hoped his instincts had been wrong. Having seen the murder scene and vision of the past, he now knew the Ripper had indeed returned and it was his duty to honour the oath he had made to Death.

A forgotten sentinel.

Recruited by Death.

To protect humanity from evil.

His escape had simply returned him to his duty.

The Raven was born from a long-standing idea that finally found a home as a screenplay. Developed initially as a TV Pilot, "Origins" is currently under consideration for adaptation to the silver screen. Designed to reflect a limited run or multi-season series, the adventures and journey of *The Raven* will reflect an episodic process with a number of novellas representing each individual "episode" as it were.

The idea will be to release a total of six episodes in the first season with the last instalment being a feature-length addition, or season finale as it were. For that reason, you will be able to purchase each individual episode on its own or else in trilogy parts or the complete story in one edition.

You can find out more about the future of *The Raven* at **WWW.TOBEY-ALEXANDER.COM/RAVEN** where you can also see some exclusive concept artwork that accompanies the pitch and series bibles delivered to studio executives for their consideration.

To continue the story, the series will be split into two parts with **three episodes** in each book going forward. I look forward to seeing you in the continuing adventures as we explore together the afterlife and the shadows we dare not normally look into.

ORDER NOW

GET THE NEXT EPISODES NOW

https://books2read.com/TheRaven1-3

ORDER NOW

COMPLETE THE SERIES NOW

https://books2read.com/TheRaven4-6

YOU'VE TAKEN YOUR FIRST STEPS INTO THIS WORLD, NOW IT'S TIME TO CONTINUE THAT JOURNEY.
THE RAVEN'S STORY CONTINUES...

11

—— · ——

BONUS ARTWORK

What follows are some early concept sketches for scenes within the book. See if you can't picture these moments in the story you've just enjoyed.

Kimberley Mansfield's part in the chess-game of John's return to his position as The Raven cannot be understated. Very much ignorant to the world she is about to encounter, Kimberley is quick to dismiss John's stories and stories from a broken mind.

We see her here as a busy graduate with only her thesis on her mind. WHat she doesn't know is her encounter with John Smith will forever change her future and her understanding of the world.

A natural reaction to her exploration of John's past is to *run*. The terror of what she has encountered is expressed here in a simple yet compelling view of her turning from John and fleeing in terror. Such a simple interaction becomes the foundation of a new experience and understanding of the world.

The Raven's birth is an aspect of the story that means so much.
Not only do we need to know the Raven's source and birth,
but how he stands as a broken emblem of what he once was.
The Raven's birth from Death is shown here in an image that
captures the strength and power of a man becoming, something

more.

The look on Kimberley's face here is important to show her acceptance of what she has done. By now you have seen her part and the willingness in which she stepped into this new world. Even in the three images of her contained here, we see an evolution of strength and resolve in a character from such a simple interaction.

The Raven in Origins is a curious dichotomy, we see the power of his creation but we also see him in the modern world disconnected and somewhat broken from his oath. With Origins, the essence of the Raven's evolution is one of *potential*.

Printed in Great Britain
by Amazon

29725798R00063